y wool
itchy.
One of our shepherds may be a wolf.
I want to be a wolf someday!

For information address HarperCollins Children's Books, a division of HarperCollins Publishers, 10 East 53rd Street, New York, NY 10022. www.harpercollinschildrens.com

Library of Congress Cataloging-in-Publication Data
Levine, Gail Carson.
Betsy Red Hoodie / by Gail Carson Levine ; illustrated by Scott Nash. — 1st ed.
p. cm.
Summary: In this variation of "Little Red Riding Hood," Betsy Red Hoodie goes to visit her grandma with her friend Zimmo the wolf and her flock of sheep, but things do not go exactly as Betsy had planned.
ISBN 978-0-06-146870-4 (trade bdg.) — ISBN 978-0-06-146871-1 (lib. bdg.)
[1. Wolves—Fiction. 2. Grandmothers—Fiction. 3. Surprise—Fiction.] I. Nash, Scott, date. II. Title.
PZ7.L578345Bb 2010
[E]—dc22
2008027456
CIP
AC

10 11 12 13 14 SCP 10 9 8 7 6 5 4 3 2 1 Designed by Dana Fritts. ❖ First Edition

Gail Carson Levine

Illustrated by Scott Nash

Betsy Red Hoodie

HARPER
An Imprint of HarperCollins*Publishers*

FLOUR
FLOUR

"Betsy, take these cupcakes to Grandma,"
Betsy's mom said. "You're old enough now."

Betsy grinned. All right! Today she was old enough to go by herself. “But what about the sheep?” Betsy was one of the shepherds of Bray Valley.

“Take them. They’ll enjoy the walk.”

Betsy opened the sheep’s pen.

Zimmo popped out of his house. He was Bray Valley’s other shepherd.

“You have to stay home,” Betsy said. “Wolves aren’t good for grandmas.” Long ago a wolf had eaten a grandma.

Pleeeee...eee...ease...

Betsy thought about it. Zimmo had never hurt a person or a sheep. "Okay. You can come."

Zimmo howled his happy herding howl, *Waa paa wooo.*

Farmer Woolsey asked Betsy where she was going.

"To Grandma's."

"With your wolf?"

"Zimmo is a good wolf!"

Zimmo howled, *Aii yii yam.*

"Be careful," Farmer Woolsey said. "He doesn't look good to me."

He's just hungry.
Maybe he's in a B-A-A-A-D mood.
Cows say mood. Is he a cow?

Beyond the farms a ram strayed from the path. Zimmo herded him and came back with daisies. He gave Betsy the daisies and ran off for more.

Betsy and the sheep picked daisies too.

The two shepherds led the sheep up Highandry Slope.

A hunter stepped out of a thicket.

Betsy jumped in front of Zimmo. "We're the shepherds of Bray Valley."

The hunter lowered his rifle. "Where are you going?"

"To my grandma's house."

Zimmo licked his lips.

"That wolf might eat your grandma. And you. Be careful."

Rosentall Mountain loomed ahead.

Zimmo ran into the woods.

Betsy shouted, “Come back!”

Zimmo grinned wolfishly and didn’t come back.

“Zimmo!” Betsy yelled. Was he trying to get to Grandma’s first? Did he really want to eat Grandma? Was the hunter right?

She blew her wolf whistle. But nobody came.

Tooo-da-looo!
One shepherd down.
Shoo, shepherd!
What shoe?

What do grandmas look like?
They have big eyes, the better to see you with.
They have long arms, the better to hug you with.
They are long in the tooth, the better to chew with.

What do wolves look like?
They have big eyes, the better to see you with.
They have long arms, the better to hug you with.
They have long teeth.
They look a lot like grandmas!

Betsy had to protect Grandma!

A lamb was missing.

The sheep stopped. Betsy looked up the path ahead and down the path behind.

No lamb.

She combed through the sheep.

No lamb.

Zimmo could be far ahead by now!

Betsy found the lamb sitting in a tree.

Rain poured down.

The sheep refused to move in the rain.

Betsy pushed the sheep. She shoved them. She pulled the wool over their eyes and yanked. She begged. She pleaded. Zimmo would have nipped their heels.

Didn't he miss her?

At last the sky cleared. The flock started up Slippenfall Hill. The path was muddy. Oh, no! Halfway up, all the sheep slid to the bottom.

Not a single lamb, ewe, or ram could go up the hill without help. Betsy had to haul them one by one. Zimmo would have helped her.

Had he forgotten they were best friends?

Betsy saw Grandma's house in the valley beyond Slippenfall Hill. The lights were out! Was Grandma—

Betsy raced, and the sheep came tumbling after her.

Betsy shoved open the door.

"Surprise!"

There was Grandma! And Mom! And Farmer Woolsey! And all the farmers of Bray Valley!

And there was Zimmo!

He ran to Betsy, tugging a gray wolf with him.

Mom said, "Meet Zimmo's grandma. She lives here on Rosentall Mountain."

Betsy gave Zimmo's grandma a cupcake. Zimmo and his grandma howled, *Haa-pee dayayay.*

Everyone said, "Happy birthday, Betsy!"

I won't help.
She'll never blow them all out.
I wonder what her wish is.
More of us.
For the cake to turn to grass.
To be a sheep someday.

For more days as good as this!

The moral is: Wolves are good for grandmas.
Some wolves are grandmas.
I'm a grandma
Am I a wolf?

Some grandmas are sheep.
Some books never end.